The Camel's Hump of Doom

PAUL COOPER

Illustrated by Trevor Dunton

PUFFIN

PUFFIN BOOKS

Published by the Penguin Group
Penguin Books Ltd, 80 Strand, London WC2R 0RL, England
Penguin Group (USA) Inc., 375 Hudson Street, New York, New York 10014, USA
Penguin Group (Canada), 90 Eglinton Avenue East, Suite 700, Toronto, Ontario, Canada M4P 2Y3
(a division of Pearson Penguin Canada Inc.)
Penguin Ireland, 25 St Stephen's Green, Dublin 2, Ireland (a division of Penguin Books Ltd)
Penguin Group (Australia), 250 Camberwell Road, Camberwell, Victoria 3124, Australia
(a division of Pearson Australia Group Pty Ltd)
Penguin Books India Pvt Ltd, 11 Community Centre, Panchsheel Park, New Delhi – 110 017, India
Penguin Group (NZ), 67 Apollo Drive, Rosedale, North Shore 0632, New Zealand
(a division of Pearson New Zealand Ltd)
Penguin Books (South Africa) (Pty) Ltd, 24 Sturdee Avenue, Rosebank, Johannesburg 2196, South Africa

Penguin Books Ltd, Registered Offices: 80 Strand, London WC2R 0RL, England

puffinbooks.com

First published 2011
001 – 10 9 8 7 6 5 4 3 2 1

Text copyright © Paul Cooper, 2011
Illustrations copyright © Trevor Dunton, 2011
All rights reserved

The moral right of the author and illustrator has been asserted

Set in Bembo Infant
Made and printed in England by Clays Ltd, St Ives plc

British Library Cataloguing in Publication Data
A CIP catalogue record for this book is available from the British Library

ISBN: 978–0–141–33210–9

www.greenpenguin.co.uk

The Camel's Hump of Doom

Pigs CAN fly!
Kweeeeeeeeeeeeeeeeeeeeeeeep!
When the Alarm Squeal sounds it must
be a job for Captain Peter Porker and
the PIGS IN PLANES!

Paul Cooper is from Manchester.
He now lives in Cambridge with
his wife and two daughters.

*Read these high-flying adventures
about the Pigs in Planes:*

Pigs in Planes: The Chicken Egg-splosion

Pigs in Planes: The Shark Bites Back

Pigs in Planes: The Big Baad Sheep

Pigs in Planes: The Mega Monkey Mystery

Pigs in Planes: The Camel's Hump of Doom

Pigs in Planes: The Big Bear Nightmare

For Cleo and Cleo's

MEET THE CREW

PEREGRINE OINKS-GRUNTINGTON,

Wing Commander

LOLA PENN,

Radio Operator

PETER PORKER,

Captain

TAMMY SNUFFLES,

Mechanic

BRIAN TROTTER,

Medical Officer

CURLY McHOGLET,

Trainee

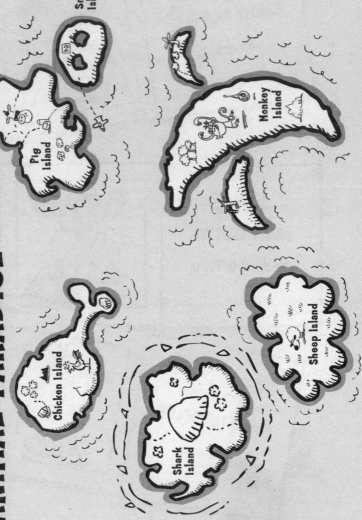

CAMEL ISLAND

Bear Island

CHAPTER 1:

A Spot of Trouble

'Ooh, it says here that I'm going to have a spot of trouble this week.' Tammy frowned as she read out her horoscope from the newspaper. 'Wonder what that's all about. I must tell Lola – she's the same star sign as me.'

The team was in the common room at the Pigs in Planes HQ. The mechanic had turned to her favourite page of *The Daily Moon* – Mystic Moggy's horoscopes.

'What star sign are you, Pete?' she asked the captain.

Pete was lovingly styling his hair, but he

tore his eyes from the
mirror. 'Leo.'

Tammy read out
the Leo horoscope. 'It
says, *You will get ahead
this week.*'

Pete didn't seem surprised. 'Cool!'
He went back to his gel.

Curly looked up
from his comic. 'What
about me, Tammy?'
the trainee PiP asked
eagerly.

'Let's see. Hmm . . . It says: *You will meet
a tall stranger. But be careful not to give him the
hump.*'

Curly was confused. 'What
does *that* mean? *Give him the
HUMP?*'

From the other side
of the room Brian 'the

Brain' Trotter let out a heavy sigh. The medical officer let out lots of these whenever Tammy was reading the horoscopes aloud. He didn't believe in astrology at all.

'*To have the hump with someone or something: to be annoyed or cross with them,*' he said, sounding exactly like the Hogsford English Dictionary. '*To give someone the hump: to make them cross or annoyed; to irritate them.*' He glared at Tammy's newspaper. 'For example, you might "give someone the hump" by reading aloud mumbo-jumbo that has absolutely NO basis in science.'

Tammy rolled her eyes. 'Typical Aries,' she said. 'They *never* believe in horoscopes.'

She took a chomp of doughnut. 'I'm going to read your horoscope out anyway, Brian. It says, *This week you will need to change your trousers unexpectedly.*'

'What nonsense!' muttered Brian. As he said this, there was the sound of trottersteps clacking along the corridor outside. The door burst open and Lola Penn rushed in.

The radio operator was wearing a green wig and her funkiest rock-star clothes because that night she was going to a fancy-dress party. But something was wrong – she had both trotters clamped over her snout and a wild look in her eye.

'What's the matter, Lola?' asked Tammy.

'SPOTTTTTTTTTTTTTTTTTTTTT-TTTTTTTT!' roared Lola. 'How can I go to a party with *this* on my nose?' She lifted one trotter to reveal a small red spot in the middle of her snout, then added: 'WAAAAAAAAAARRGGHHH!!'

Brian jerked back and the teacup in his trotter toppled and fell from its saucer.

'See, Brian?' Tammy chuckled. 'Now you need to change your trousers because you've spilt tea on them! Your horoscope came true.'

A satisfied smile played on Brian's face.

'Actually, I spilt tea all down my *shirt*, and not on my *trousers* at all, thank you.' Then he realized that there was still tea all over his nice clean shirt, and his smile wobbled a bit.

Meanwhile Curly pointed to Lola, who had elbowed Pete aside from the mirror so she could get a better look at the spot.

'Brian's horoscope might not have come true but Lola *has* got a spot of trouble,' the trainee said.

'WAAAAAAAAAAAAARRRGHHH!'
agreed Lola.

While Lola got ready for her party, Wing
Commander Peregrine Oinks-Gruntington
had promised to stay by the radio.
He was quite surprised when someone
called.

'Pigs in Planes rescue service,' he said,
picking up the microphone. 'State your
name, species and the nature of the problem.'

He was even more surprised to find that
the voice on the other end of the line was
one he knew. 'Peregrine? Is that *you*?'

'Howard?' The wing
commander had
just started wearing
a glass monocle
in one eye; this
popped out in
surprise now.

Howard Oinks-Gruntington, the wing commander's younger brother, was an archaeologist – he spent most of his time digging up old bones and bits of pottery.

'What trouble have you gone and got yourself into this time?' Peregrine asked.

'I'm sort of a little bit . . . stuck in the middle of the desert,' said Howard. 'My jeep won't go. I was wondering if someone could pick me up?'

'We're an emergency rescue agency,' grumbled Peregrine, 'not a minicab service.'

'It IS a bit of an emergency, actually, Peregrine,' said his brother. 'There's no food and no water, and I think there's a sandstorm coming.'

It was the PiPs' policy never to pass judgement on a caller, but Peregrine couldn't stop himself. 'That was a bit twitty, wasn't it?' he said to the pig he would forever think of as his annoying little brother.

He expected Howard to say something rude back – that was how the two of them usually communicated – but all he heard on the radio was a strange *THUD*, then a noise like something heavy falling to the ground. It sounded a bit like someone dropping a bowling ball on to a bag of flour, then throwing a sack of spuds off a truck. Or maybe like a pig being hit on the head and then falling to the ground.

'Howard?' he said. 'Are you still there? Have you forgotten how to operate a radio now?'

All Peregrine could hear was someone spitting – it didn't *sound* like his brother. Then there was the sound of someone chuckling – that *definitely* didn't sound like Howard, who had a much more annoying laugh, in Peregrine's opinion.

And then the radio clicked off.

'Howard?' said the wing commander into the silence. 'Howard? Where ARE you?'

CHAPTER 2:

Head in the Sand

*KWEEEEEEEEEEEEEEEEEEEEEEEEEEE-
EEEEEEEEEEEEEEP!*

The Alarm Squeal rang all around the
PiPs base. As the team charged for the door,
Pete called to Lola, 'You can hardly see that
spot on your nose, you know.'

'You can see it from SPACE!' wailed the
radio operator.

The PiPs were surprised to find the wing
commander already outside waiting for
them. Somehow he had managed to squeeze
his bulk into a PiPs operational flightsuit.

'Tammy and Brian, you stay here with

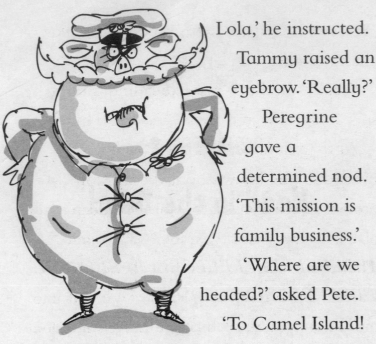

Lola,' he instructed. Tammy raised an eyebrow. 'Really?' Peregrine gave a determined nod. 'This mission is family business.' 'Where are we headed?' asked Pete. 'To Camel Island! We're going to the desert!'

Minutes later, the PiPs were flying south towards Camel Island. Curly rode with Pete in SkyHog 1, while Peregrine took the controls of Brian's plane.

'Careful, Peregrine,' said Pete over the radio. 'You're wobbling a bit. It's been a while since you've flown a SkyHog jet, you know.'

'Nonsense!' said the wing commander.

'You never forget how to fly – it's just like riding a bike!'

'Yeah,' said Pete, 'just like riding a high-speed, fuel-injected, rocket-powered bike!'

As they flew, Peregrine explained everything he knew about the mission. 'My brother is on a team looking for the hidden tomb of the ancient Camel Pharaoh Nokankumin. They've been digging near the Valley of the Camel Kings. Apparently, Howard went off into the desert to check out a new lead. Now he's gone and got himself stranded without any provisions or transport.' He tutted. 'Typical Howard – always got his head in the sand. He's spent years looking for Nokankumin's tomb, and he *still* hasn't found it. Can't be looking hard enough, if you ask me.'

'But Lola says YOU can't find your own underpants without a map of the area,' said Curly, scratching his head.

'What's that, McHoglet?'

'Nothing, sir.' The trainee PiP glanced out of the window. They had flown beyond the cities that clung to the coastline of Camel Island. Now they were coming to the edge of the enormous desert. Curly looked eagerly at all the lovely yellow sand dunes below, stretching for miles in every direction.

It wasn't long before they reached the right coordinates and spotted the abandoned jeep in the sand below.

'See?' muttered the wing commander. '*Always* got his head in the sand.'

The PiPs landed their jets on the nearest stretch of level ground and then raced out into the heat of the desert.

Not far from the jeep, there was a shallow pit with a string roping it off, a small pop-up tent and several other items lying around . . . but no sign of Howard.

While Pete went to check the tent, Peregrine looked over the abandoned jeep.

'I love sand!' cried Curly, hopping up and down with excitement. 'Can we build a sandcastle when we've found your brother? Can we? Huh?'

'Don't be so silly, McHoglet!' said the wing commander, wondering where on earth his brother could have got to. 'You haven't even got a spade!'

Curly pulled a little red plastic spade out of his back pocket. 'My nan sent me one!'

'Put it away!' said Peregrine. 'Anyway, there's no point having a spade with no bucket!'

But Curly just pointed to an upturned bucket a few metres away.

'I can use *that*!' he said. He charged over and picked the bucket up.

'EEK!' he cried, slamming it back down again.

'What's wrong, lad?'

The young pig had gone a pale shade of pink with just a touch of green round the edges. 'There's . . . a *head* underneath this bucket.'

'*What?* Show me!' demanded Peregrine.

With trembling trotters, Curly lifted the bucket again. It was true – there, underneath the bucket, was a pig's head.

Its eyes seemed almost to be looking up at them from the sand.

'It's horrible, isn't it?' gasped Curly.

'*Dreadful!*' agreed Peregrine, looking down at the head. 'Do you actually call that thing above your lip a *moustache*, Howard?'

CHAPTER 3:

Mummies for Dummies

Back at PIPs HQ, Lola was frantically looking for an alternative fancy-dress costume – one that would cover the spot on her snout.

'How about this one?' she asked.

'Pardon?' said Brian.

Lola opened up the front panel of the gigantic metal deep-sea diving helmet she was wearing now. 'I said, how about this costume?'

Tammy shook her head. 'I don't think you'll be able to dance much in that, Lola.'

The radio operator wandered off to look

for something else.

Meanwhile Tammy had some questions for Brian. 'Who was this Nokankumin character anyway?'

The PiPs medic tried to hide the hurt look in his eyes. 'Didn't you read the book I got you for your birthday? *Mummies for Dummies – Everything You Ever Wanted to Know About the Ancient Pharaohs of Camel Island, Plus Quite a Lot More*? It had a whole chapter on Nokankumin.'

'Yes, yes, of course I read that,' lied Tammy. 'It was brilliant. But . . . erm . . . just remind me of the main bits.'

Brian sighed. 'Thousands of years ago Camel Island was ruled by powerful camel pharaohs. They built the pyramids.'

'What, all by themselves?' asked Tammy.

'Well, no, they didn't actually roll up their sleeves and lug all those gigantic stones across the desert themselves. They had armies of animal slaves to do it for them. The pharaohs were very powerful, and the most powerful of all was Nokankumin. According to legend, he claimed that he was more powerful even than the gods themselves.'

Tammy nodded. 'I get the picture. He ordered everyone about, didn't do a lick of work himself and was a bighead. I had a boss like that once!' She glanced at a photo of Peregrine on the office wall. 'Come to think of it, I still do!'

Brian continued explaining about

Nokankumin. 'When they died, the pharaohs were buried in huge tombs in the desert with lots of treasures all around them. Over the centuries, grave robbers have stolen everything from these tombs . . . all except Nokankumin's. Nobody has ever found it, but from what I understand, Howard Oinks-Gruntington and his team are close to discovering it at last.'

'Cool!' said Tammy.

'And then finally, animals can stop going on and on about the Curse of Nokankumin's Tomb,' continued Brian.

Tammy froze. 'What did you say? A CURSE? What curse?'

'Supposedly, terrible things are meant to happen to any intruder who disturbs the tomb of Nokankumin.' Brian smiled. 'Silly, isn't it?'

But Tammy was already on her trotters and running towards the radio.

'What are you doing?' the medic asked her.

'I'm checking the others are OK!' she cried.

Brian blinked in confusion. 'Tammy, I can assure you that on a simple mission like this, absolutely nothing bad is going to happen to anyone on the team.'

Brian had absolutely no idea just how wrong he was . . .

To Curly's relief, the pig's head on the sand wasn't *just* a pig's head. Well, it was – but it was also attached to a pig's body, which had been buried in the sand. Specifically, the head belonged to Howard Oinks-Gruntington, famous archaeologist and younger brother of Peregrine Oinks-Gruntington.

Howard glared up at his big brother. 'Are you going to stand there all day with that silly-looking monocle and that ridiculously oversized moustache, or are you going to get me out of here?'

Peregrine frowned. 'You always were an ungrateful little porker, Howard, even when we were piglets.' He turned to Curly. 'Dig him out, would you, young McHoglet?'

Happily, Curly got to work. 'I *knew* it was

a good idea to bring a spade!'

The wing commander looked towards the tent and shouted, 'What are you doing over there, Captain Porker? We've found Howard!' As Curly continued to dig, Peregrine turned and asked, 'So how did you go and get yourself in a mess like this, Howard?'

'Ptt–pttt–ppppt–owf!' replied the younger Oinks-Gruntington.

'Speak up!' boomed Peregrine. 'You always were a mumbler!'

Howard spat some more. 'I said, please tell this piglet not to throw sand in my mouth!'

'Oops – sorry!' said Curly.

'Well, Howard?' said Peregrine impatiently. 'You didn't answer the question!'

'Pffff-ta-DOO!' said Howard through another mouthful of sand.

'Oops – sorry again!'

Howard spat more sand out, then cried,

'I said, BEHIND YOU!'

Both Peregrine and Curly looked round, just in time for their brains to register that the tent seemed to have moved closer. Then Peregrine noticed that behind it, Pete was lying unconscious on the sand.

'What the —'

Before he could say more, the tent shot forward and something sprang out of it — a camel!

Like all of its kind, it had big heavy hoofs. These help camels walk long distances across the sandy wastes of the desert. They're also really good for clopping pigs on the head and knocking them out.

And that is exactly what this camel did.

CHAPTER 4:

HEADS in the Sand

When they woke up, Pete, Curly and Peregrine didn't feel too good. For one thing, the sun was beating down on them without mercy.

But to make matters worse, they too had been buried up to their necks in the sand, right next to Howard. The four pigs' heads were lined up like a neat row of cabbages. They all pointed out towards mile after mile of shifting sand dunes and slowly baked in the sun.

'I wonder if this is what the horoscope meant when it said you'd "get ahead",' said

Curly glumly.

Peregrine wasn't glum; he was cross. 'You could have given us a warning, Howard,' he grumbled.

'I believe most pigs would consider the words "Behind you!" a fair warning, *Peregrine*,' said Howard tartly.

'You haven't even said thank you for coming to your rescue, *yet again*,' complained the wing commander.

'Yes, of course . . . Thank you for coming along and getting yourself buried in the sand alongside me. Otherwise I don't know what I would have done – been buried in the sand alone?'

'You ungrateful hog!' spat Peregrine.

'Big Nose!' replied Howard.

'Oh, trust you to revert to childish name-calling,' said Peregrine. 'Well, two can play at that game . . . *Chicken Legs!*'

'Big Nose!'

'Chicken Legs!'

'Big Nose!'

'Chicken Legs!

'It's always nice to catch up with family,' Pete cut in, 'but perhaps we should be thinking about our present situation?'

'Quite so,' agreed Peregrine. 'And my *baby* brother can start by telling us who that camel was!'

Howard sighed. 'His name is Tom – Tom Braider – and he was one of my team searching for the hidden tomb of Nokankumin.'

'People have been looking for that for years, haven't they?' chipped in Curly. 'We saw a DVD about it at school.'

'Over the centuries many have tried and found nothing more than an empty chamber,' said Howard. 'But I was able to translate an ancient scroll from the Piggish Museum. It spoke of a special key that can open the tomb's secret entrance.'

'What sort of key?' asked Curly.

'A camel's hump made of jet-black stone. That's what Tom and I came to this second site to find . . . and we DID! We found Nokankumin's legendary Hump of Doom! We were about to drive back to the main dig site when I discovered the jeep had been tampered with. Worse still, the water was all gone. I tried to radio the rest of the team at the dig site, but I couldn't get through. That's when I called you, Peregrine. But as soon as I'd put the radio down, something clobbered me from behind. I only found out it was Tom when he clobbered you, too.'

'So now Tom's got the hump?' asked Peregrine.

'He's not the only one,' said Pete. '*I've* got the hump about being buried up to my neck in sand.'

Suddenly, Curly piped up from the end of the row. 'Excuse me! Can I just ask a quick question? Beetles have got six legs, haven't they?'

'Yes,' said Howard.

'OK, thanks . . . And spiders have got eight legs?'

'Correct.'

'But they haven't got pincers or nasty-looking stingers at the end of their tails?'

'Of course not! Why?'

'Well . . .'

Curly didn't need to say any more because that's when the scorpion wandered into the other pigs' line of vision.

It stopped and turned towards them. Life was pretty dull for a young scorpion out here in the desert, so a row of four gigantic pig heads like this was big news.

Four pairs of wide-open piggy eyes watched as the creature waved its deadly stinger gently in the hot air, as if to say,

'Eeny, meeny, miney, mo,
On which big piggy's head shall I go?'

★ ★ ★

'Hello? Hello? Will someone please answer?'

Back at PiPs HQ, Tammy was trying to get through to the team by radio. It was her third attempt and there was still no answer.

She gave Brian a worried look. 'It isn't like Pete not to answer a call.' She thought about this. 'Well, OK . . . it IS exactly like Pete, but it isn't like Curly or Peregrine. What if something's gone wrong?'

In situations like this, Brian prided himself on staying calm and professional. 'I'm *positive* nothing has gone wrong,' he said. 'I bet they report back in a few minutes.'

'You do know that Peregrine has taken your plane, don't you?' asked Tammy.

'WHAT?' Brian leapt to his trotters. 'What are we waiting for? Let's fly over there RIGHT NOW and see what's happening!'

He started rifling through the papers in

front of the radio on Lola's desk. 'Where are the mission coordinates? Lola always logs the mission coordinates! We need the mission coordinates!'

'It was *Peregrine* who took the emergency call,' said Tammy. 'He's not very good at details, like writing things down. But don't worry – we can work out their position from their last radio message as they reached the desert. It should get us close enough.'

As they rushed towards the door, a horrible-looking monster popped its head round the corner.

'AAAARGH!' screamed Brian.

'Hmm,' said Tammy calmly. 'You

won't be able to eat any of the nibbles at the party with that monster mask on, Lola.'

The radio operator glumly pulled the rubber mask off and watched as the two PiPs ran towards the runway.

CHAPTER 5:

The Song of the Desert

In the desert, only one of the four buried piggies kept his cool.

This wasn't easy with a scorpion heading his way, but 'Keeping Calm in Moments of High Danger' was on Captain Peter Porker's top ten list of hobbies (just behind 'Doing Insanely Extreme Sports' and ahead of 'Playing Tiddlywinks for Cash').

He angled his head towards the wing commander next to him. 'Peregrine! That new monocle of yours is always popping out, isn't it? See if you can pop it out in my direction!'

'What? Why?' spluttered Peregrine.

The scorpion started to move slowly in their direction.

'Just do it!' cried Pete.

Craning his neck towards the PiPs captain, Peregrine squeezed the muscles around his right eye – *squeeze, relax, squeeze, relax*. The pressure built up and up until . . . POP! The monocle shot out like a cork from a bottle.

Knowing that he wouldn't have another chance, Pete jerked his neck and – *got it!* – he caught the monocle between his teeth.

Carefully, he moved it forward with his tongue until it poked straight out from his lips.

'What's going on?' asked Howard, unable to see what the captain was up to.

As Pete moved his snout, a tiny dot of light tracked across the sand in front of him. It was the sun's rays focused into a tight and powerful beam through the lens of Peregrine's monocle.

Pete tilted his head some more, and now the dot of light was on the scorpion's tail. After a few seconds, a tiny plume of smoke appeared.

Suddenly, the scorpion hopped up into the air, clacking its pincers wildly. This was understandable given that its bum had caught fire. It put the flames out in the sand and scurried off crossly.

'Well played, Porker!' boomed Peregrine. Then to Howard he added, 'What were you saying about how silly monocles look, hmm?'

'You haven't changed one bit, have you, Peregrine?' replied Howard. 'Not from the tip of your ears down to the little curly tail on your big fat b—'

'If you two can stop squabbling for two minutes,' cut in Pete, 'we'd better think about getting out of here . . . Any ideas?'

Nobody spoke, but they became aware of a series of grunts coming from the end of the line of heads – from Curly.

'What are you doing, Trainee McHoglet?' asked Peregrine.

The grunting and panting stopped. 'Trying to escape, sir,' said Curly. 'When I was a piglet, my big sister buried me in the sand on the beach every year, then decorated my head with shells. Eventually I worked out a way of escaping. I just had to fill my chest with air and hold my breath when the sand was going in around me. Then later I could make room by breathing out, and then just sort of *wriggle* my way free. I got pretty good at it, actually!'

'So why can't you just do it now?' asked Pete.

'I'm not sure,' murmured Curly. 'Unless . . . Well, there IS one thing that's different. When we were at the beach, my nan always used to sing, "I Do Like to Be Beside the Seaside" to us. Maybe if you all sang that while I tried to get out . . .?'

Nobody was too keen on this idea, but

they were even less keen on becoming hog roasts. The three pigs began to sing flatly while Curly went back to wriggling like the world's plumpest pink worm.

'It's not working,' he said after a while. 'My nan's voice was higher than that, and more . . . *squawky*.'

The three other pigs took up the song again, higher and squawkier now.

'That's better!' said Curly, and he resumed wiggling his body in the sand. 'I've almost got one trotter out!'

As the other pigs continued their song, they became aware of something moving in front of them. The little scorpion was back, but this time it wasn't alone. It had brought its big brother with it.

'Keep singing!' cried Curly. 'I'm almost out of here!'

The other three pigs went on with the fastest, most terrified version of 'I Do Like to Be Beside the Seaside' in the history of popular music.

The bigger scorpion was right in front of Peregrine now, its pincers almost touching him. It looked up at the giant moustache waving over its head. Something about the wing commander's singing seemed to anger it. Its stinger hovered at the ready . . .

'Don't worry, sir!' cried Curly, shooting his arms up in a shower of sand. With his trotters free, he could scramble out of his sandy prison. But was he too late? The big scorpion had arched its back, its stinger set to strike at Peregrine . . . Curly swept up the spade and thrust it between the scorpion's stinger and Peregrine's face. The stinger jabbed harmlessly against the red plastic.

With a quick flick of his wrist Curly used the spade to bat the scorpion back towards its little chum. Then he gripped the spade in one hand like a weapon.

'Don't even *think* about coming near
these pigs,' he snarled in his best tough-pig
voice. Then he added in a voice that wasn't
quite so tough: 'Not that you probably do a
lot of thinking, what with being scorpions.
But . . . erm . . . if you *were* thinking about it
. . . well then, DON'T! Think about, that is
. . . if you get my meaning . . . which you
don't . . . probably.'

'That's easy for you to say, kid,' Pete commented.

The scorpions turned their pinprick eyes on the large creature before them. They quickly decided that they didn't want to mess with anything quite so . . . weird. So with one last snap of the pincers, they turned and legged it away into the sand.

'Good work, Curly!' said Peregrine.

'Indeed!' said Howard. 'Good work, everybody! It's just a pity that one of us was out of tune. But then, you never were a very good singer, were you, brother?'

CHAPTER 6:

What's in a Name?

The passenger seat in Tammy's plane, the 'Sty in the Sky', was so full of sweetie wrappers and pizza boxes that there was no room for Brian. Instead they took the larger PiPs cargo plane, with Tammy at the wheel.

As they zoomed towards Camel Island, Brian noticed that Tammy's backpack was even more full than usual.

'What have you got in there?' he asked.

'Important desert provisions,' Tammy said.

As they flew, they continued trying to contact the others by radio, but with no success. Soon they reached Camel Island,

and not long after that they were flying low over the desert.

'Based on their last call, we shouldn't be too far from them,' said Tammy. She started to fly in a standard PiPs search pattern.

'I don't see what chance we have of finding *anything* in this desert,' sighed Brian. 'It's like looking for a needle in a haystack the size of Jupiter!'

Ignoring the medic, Tammy cried, 'I can see someone . . . and he's waving at us!'

She brought the plane lower to get a better look at the large figure below. 'That isn't a pig,' she said. 'It's a camel! I'm going to see if he knows anything about the others.'

As the plane landed on a flat patch, it created a mini-sandstorm, but the camel didn't mind. Like all camels, he had long eyelashes to protect his eyes against flying sand. He could even close his nostrils to stop sand getting up them.

When the plane's door opened, he arranged his face into a smile. 'Got room for one more?' he called in the friendliest voice he could manage.

'OK,' answered Tammy. 'What's your name?'

'Tom,' answered the camel. 'Tom Braider.'

As he walked to the plane, he gripped his canvas bag tightly. The last thing he wanted to do was lose the Hump of Doom.

Curly was digging the other pigs out of the sand with his trusty spade. As he worked, he had another question for Howard. 'What did you say Tom's last name was, Mr Oinks-Gruntington?'

With half of his body free, Howard was able to dodge the scoopfuls of sand flying his way. 'Braider. Why?'

Curly frowned. 'So his name is "Tom Braider"?'

'Yes!' Howard said, pulling himself up and dusting off his khaki desert suit. 'What of it? I fail to see how this helps our situation.'

'For once I agree with my brother,' said

Peregrine. 'There are more important things to discuss, McHoglet.'

Curly was digging out the wing commander now. 'Well, it's just . . . if you move the B over, TOM BRAIDER makes the words TOMB RAIDER. Isn't that a bit of an odd name for an archaeologist?'

There was an awkward silence, then a series of guffaws erupted from Peregrine. 'Oh, that is priceless! Howard, you have been fooled by a tomb raider going by the name of TOMB RAIDER!'

Peregrine was still chuckling when all of the pigs were free of their sandy prison.

'Perhaps we ought to think about what that camel's going to do when he reaches the dig site,' said Pete.

'He'll be able to use the Hump of Doom to find the hidden tomb and rob everything,' said Howard bleakly.

'Not if we get there first,' said Peregrine.

'We can beat him there easily in the planes.'

There was just one tiny problem, which Pete soon discovered when he went over to examine the jets. 'We're not going anywhere in these. That camel has smashed up all the control panels.'

'What about the radios?' asked Howard. 'You can call the other members of your team.'

Pete tried the radio and at first it seemed OK. After a couple of moments, the voice of the PiPs mechanic came over loud and clear.

'Pete! Where have you been?'

Pete started explaining everything, but then Tammy spoke again.

'Hello, Pete? Are you there? You must be, but I can't hear you.'

Pete slammed his trotter against the broken radio in anger. They could still receive messages, but they couldn't send any.

'Don't worry,' Tammy said breezily.
'Brian and I have flown over to the island
ourselves. Nice here, innit? We've just picked
up Howard's camel friend, Tom.'

'No!' shouted Curly. 'That rotten camel
attacked us and left us to roast in the desert!'
But of course Tammy and Brian couldn't
hear him.

'Not to worry,' continued Tammy. 'Tom has told us you're all OK and you've flown Howard to the main dig site. So hopefully see you there. OK, byeeeeeee!'

'No, Tammy, wait!' shouted Pete, but it was no use. There was a CLICK! as she broke the connection.

'So let me get this straight . . .' Howard Oinks-Gruntington looked pale. 'Your team-mates are giving the camel who stole the Hump and left us for dead a lift straight to the dig site!'

Peregrine wasn't laughing now. He gave his younger brother a dark look. 'How far away is this place?' he asked.

'Twenty miles.'

The wing commander tugged on his full-bodied moustache. 'We'll walk there,' he said at last. 'After all, that's what this Tom character was going to do.'

Howard wasn't convinced. 'Camels are

built for the desert. And don't forget their humps! With that great big store of fat on their backs, they can go for days on end without water. How long can WE go without water?'

'I never drink water!' chipped in Curly helpfully. 'My nan says fish wee in it.'

Peregrine was shaking his head. 'You never had any stamina, Howard, even as a piglet.'

Howard glared at his older brother. 'Right,' he snarled. 'If *you* can trek across the desert, I'm sure *I* can too.'

And with these hot words under an even hotter sun, the four pigs set off across the sea of sand.

CHAPTER 7:

Seasick

The limestone cliffs of the Valley of the Camel Kings marked the edge of the desert. Centuries ago the ancient Camels had carved tombs deep into the soft rock as burial places for their rulers.

'It's good of you to give me a lift,' said Tom the camel, still being nice and friendly to the two pigs.

Tammy narrowed her eyes. 'And you're *sure* our friends are here?' she said.

'Yes, yes! They'll be at the main dig – it's this way.'

He started to lead them through the

valley. Along the way they passed several holes carved into the limestone. Brian knew that these led to the different tombs. Over the centuries, all of those tombs had been found and emptied . . . all except one.

At the end of the valley there was a smaller hole with a tent outside it. A couple of camels were at work with digging tools at the entrance. There was no sign of the other PiPs.

'Just wait here,' said Tom, and his face twisted into that same strange smile. He cantered over to the others and began to talk in a low murmur.

'I don't like this,' whispered Tammy out of the side of her snout.

'Me neither,' replied Brian. 'I LOVE it! I can't believe we're in the Valley of the Camel Kings!'

Tom turned back to the two pigs. 'Apparently your wing commander has flown Howard to the hospital, just for a check-up. Your other team-mates went down into the tomb for a look around.'

'Really?' said Tammy. 'That doesn't sound like Pete.'

Tom's lips twisted into a smile. 'My colleagues explained it might be dangerous, but he wanted to go anyway.'

'OK, *that* sounds like Pete,' admitted Tammy.

Tom's smile twisted some more until it became one of sympathy. 'They should have

come out by now. My workers here, Dick and Drom, would have gone to search for them, but there's a narrow part at the end of the passage that's too small for a camel to get through. I don't suppose . . .?'

'We'd love to go!' Brian blurted. 'We can make sure Pete and Curly are OK, and we can have a look around. Right, Tammy?'

Tammy nodded slowly.

'Jolly good,' said Tom, opening his canvas bag. 'Then you're going to need THIS.'

A smooth black object fell out of the bag. It was round on one side and flat on the other. Its stone surface almost seemed to glow with its own dark light. It was Nokankumin's Hump of Doom.

'Now listen carefully,' said Tom, his eyes glittering. 'This is what you have to do . . .'

★ ★ ★

At first, both Oinks-Gruntingtons wanted
to be at the front of the long trek.

'I should lead the way because I know
the map coordinates,' said Howard.

'Ah, but I've got the compass,' said
Peregrine. 'And anyway, I'm the oldest!'

'Yes, but I'm the smartest!'

They both walked faster and faster,

until soon they were jogging through the
desert, elbows bumping as each brother
tried to get ahead.

'Get back here, Chicken Legs!'

'No chance, Big Nose!'

But not even the battling Oinks-
Gruntingtons could keep this up for long:

just walking in the soft sand wasn't easy,
let alone out-running your brother. Soon,
all four pigs could manage no more than
a steady plod. With the sun still high and
a sea of sand all around them, it felt as if
they would be walking forever.

'I wouldn't mind a nice long drink,'
gasped Pete.

'No probs!' said Curly, swinging the

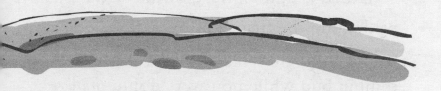

backpack off his shoulder. 'I've got food
and drink right here!'

He sat cross-legged and unbuckled
his bag, humming to himself. Then he
unscrewed the lid of his water flask and
started pouring water out on to his
trotters.

'CURLY!' shrieked Peregrine. 'What are you DOING?'

Curly looked up in surprise. 'I'm washing my trotters, sir. According to *PiPs Rules and Regulations*, you should always do that before eating. Otherwise you might pick up a nasty tummy bug.'

Peregrine looked as if he might explode. 'But we are trekking across the desert!'

'Exactly,' said Curly, glowing with pride (and the first signs of heat exhaustion). 'It would be awful to have a tummy bug while you were doing *that*!'

'Is there *any* water left?' asked Howard.

'I'm afraid not.' Curly turned the flask upside down to prove his point. In fact, there *had been* some water left, but now it spilt out on to the sand. 'Oops.'

'Not to worry, Curly,' said Pete. 'What food have you got in there?'

Curly pulled a packet out of his bag. 'Some nice ready-salted crisps!' he said brightly. 'Who wants some?'

CHAPTER 8:

A Tomb with a View

The three camels waited at the entrance to
the tunnel as Tammy and Brian went inside.
Tammy had the stone hump in her arms,
while Brian held a torch to light their way.
He ran its beam along the tunnel's walls.
There were rows of weird-looking pictures

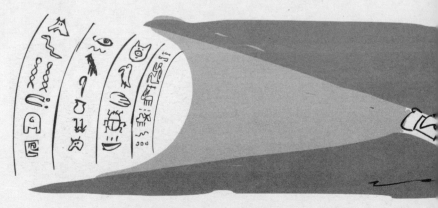

carved along them.

'Some animals will put graffiti anywhere, won't they?' Tammy tutted.

'These aren't graffiti – they're pictures of all the gods the ancients believed in,' said Brian. He pointed a few of them out. 'That one is the Jackal and there's the Hawk god. And that nice-looking one there was the ancient pig goddess, Hamm.' He turned to Tammy. 'The ancients believed in lots of gods, but Nokankumin said he was more powerful than all of them.'

A little further down the tunnel, there were rows of symbols. To Tammy, they were

just a load of old squiggles and pictures, but Brian was gazing at them. 'They're *hieroglyphics*,' he said. 'The writing of the ancients.'

'Can you read them?'

'I'm a little rusty,' said Brian, 'but I think it says, "MAY GREAT GOOD FORTUNE FALL ON THOSE WHO DISTURB THE TOMB OF THE MIGHTY PHARAOH NOKANKUMIN."'

'Ah, that's nice,' said Tammy warmly.

Brian paused. 'Oh no, wait a mo – I've translated that first bit wrongly. It doesn't say "GREAT GOOD FORTUNE", it says . . . "A TERRIBLE CURSE".'

Tammy froze. 'You said there was no such thing as the Curse of Nokankumin!' she wailed.

Brian just gave a little smile and shook his head. 'Oh, come along, Tammy. Don't tell me you've fallen for even more superstitious mumbo-jumbo, have you? There is NO such thing as a curse of the pharaoh's tomb. And anyway – OW!'

He fell to the dusty ground, clutching his head in pain.

Tammy looked down with wide eyes. 'What were you just saying?'

The medic got to his trotters and rubbed the painful bump on top of his head. 'There's a perfectly logical explanation for what just happened. I didn't see that low beam, that's all.'

Tammy wasn't convinced. 'You've never done that before, though, Brian.'

'We've never walked down this passageway before.'

Once they had squeezed their way through the narrow part, they found themselves in a small stone room.

'It's a dead end,' said Tammy. 'So where could Pete and Curly be?'

Brian was shining his torch into the chamber. In the middle of it stood a small stone statue of a camel. It didn't look quite right because something was missing – its hump.

'Remember what Tom said?' whispered Brian. 'We have to put the stone hump on to the statue.'

Tammy lifted the hump and set it down on to the flat top of the statue. It was a perfect fit.

'Now what?' asked Tammy.

'Not sure,' said Brian.

Seconds passed, and then they heard the sound of far-off rumbling.

'Did you have six helpings of rice pudding for breakfast again?' Brian asked.

'Yes, but that wasn't my tummy rumbling just now,' said Tammy.

It was true – the sound seemed to come from all around them, and it was getting louder. Soon the whole place was shaking,

and then there
was a grinding
noise as the walls
around them
began to move.
The Hump of
Doom must
have triggered
some kind of
mechanism!

'What's going
on?' cried Tammy.
'An *earthquake*?'

'I don't know!'
wailed Brian,
clutching the
mechanic's arm.
'But I'm sure
there's a logical
explanation for
it!'

When the chamber had stopped shaking and moving, Brian and Tammy were amazed to see that the walls had opened up to reveal a new doorway into a much larger chamber.

The two pigs entered it, hardly able to believe their eyes. Unlike the smaller first chamber, this one was full of statues and fancy vases and gold and jewels.

'It's the hidden tomb of Nokankumin!' gasped Brian.

'Pity they haven't got an air freshener or two,' Tammy said, sniffing. 'What about all those wardrobes propped up against the walls?'

Brian ran the torch round the walls of the circular room. Between the various stone columns and shadowy entrances to other parts of the tomb, there were six or seven tall objects. 'Those aren't wardrobes, Tammy. They're *sarcophagi*.'

'Sar-WHAT-agi?'

'They're stone coffins,' explained Brian. 'They probably contain the mummified bodies of Nokankumin's servants.' He pointed the torchlight at the biggest and most ornate of the coffins that lay flat in the middle of the room. 'And I bet *that* one contains the body of Pharaoh Nokankumin himself.' He paused. 'Er, what are you doing, Tammy?'

The mechanic had picked up one of the stone jars from the floor and was trying to unscrew the lid. 'I get hungry when I'm nervous,' she explained. 'I'm just having a quick look to see if there's anything left in these cookie jars.'

'Those aren't cookie jars!' Brian hissed. 'They're *canopic* jars. When the pharaoh died, his inside bits were removed and put into jars like that. That one probably contains a dried-up spleen or liver.'

Tammy put the jar down quickly and pulled a face. 'Dried-up spleen? Blimey, what's wrong with just keeping a few oatmeal-raisin cookies in your cookie jar?'

But Brian was looking around with wonder. 'I don't think you understand, Tammy. This is the most important archaeological discovery of modern times! Every university in Animal Paradise will want to study it. It's a treasure trove of historical information! We have to go and tell the camels.' He started towards the exit.

'Hold on,' said Tammy. 'What about Pete and Curly?'

'You needn't worry about them,' said a cold voice. 'I wasn't entirely truthful about your little friends. But I can assure you, I *have* taken care of them.'

Brian shone his torch in the direction of the voice. It lit up the long droopy face of the camel known as Tom, but he didn't

look quite so friendly now. His voice was less friendly too – less friendly and more . . . *evil*. He was blocking the exit, and Dick and Drom were behind him. When the walls of the tomb had moved, the narrow part of the entrance passage must have widened enough for them to enter.

The reflection of all the gold in the chamber shone now in the camel's dark eyes. His lips twisted into a smile, and for once it suited his face – it was a wicked sneer.

Tammy just nodded. 'I see,' she said. 'This place is a treasure trove of information, but it's also a treasure trove of TREASURE! You aren't an archaeologist at all, are you? You're here to steal the treasure. You're nothing but dirty rotten tomb raiders!'

The camels looked at each other, then smirked.

'Tomb raiders?' said the camel who had called himself Tom Braider. 'Oh no, we're much, *much* worse than that . . .'

CHAPTER 9:

Return of the Mummies

Meanwhile, the rest of the PiPs continued their slow painful journey across the sands towards the Valley of the Camel Kings.

'Look over there!' said Peregrine. 'Between that sand dune and . . . er . . . that *other* sand dune. It's a watering-hole!'

At first Pete couldn't see anything, but then the heat seemed to shimmer and he too could make something out. It looked like a small oasis with several trees and – most importantly – a lovely pool of water.

Just the thought of plunging his face into that cool water gave Pete the strength to keep going.

'Save your energy,' advised Howard.
'Whatever you think you can see, it isn't
real – it's what they call a *mirage*. The mind
plays tricks out here in the desert. There isn't
actually anything there at all.'

Sure enough, as Pete got near the spot
between the dunes, the oasis seemed to
flicker in the heat and then disappear. The
captain fell to his knees and dug his trotters
into the hot dry sand. 'NO!'

The pigs walked on in silence. After
another mile or so, Curly spotted something
else in the distance. His eyes lit up.

'It's a drinks vending machine, full of cans
of Slurpo-Pop!' he exclaimed. 'Can't you see
it?'

'No,' said Pete.

But it seemed so real to Curly. As he got
closer, he could even see the water droplets
on the outside of the machine, hear the low

hum of the machine's electricity.
He stumbled on faster and faster,
eager to get the first can.

But when he got closer, the
vending machine just seemed to
float away in the heat.

'Where's it gone?' asked Curly
in confusion.

Howard didn't stop his steady
trudge forward. 'I told you –
those mirages are tricky.'

Curly looked down at the

coins in his trotter. 'I've even got the correct change,' he mumbled.

The pigs forced their aching legs to walk on. Their whole world seemed to be made up of nothing but sand and sun, and not in a good way like in a holiday brochure.

Soon they all took turns gasping, 'Must . . . have . . . a drink!'

After a few more miles, Pete came over yet another dune and saw something else.

'What's *that*?' he said. 'It looks like an ice-cream van!'

Curly joined him, squinting into the sun's glare. 'I see it too! It's got a big plastic ice-cream cone on top.'

'Yeah! And a picture of a penguin and a sign that says "GET YOUR ICE-COLD LOLLIES"!'

The trainee shook his head. 'It's another of those rotten *mirages*, isn't it?' he said glumly.

'Yup,' Pete answered. 'Don't waste your energy running over to it, kid.'

With heads down, they staggered on.

Deep inside the hidden tomb of Nokankumin, Tammy and Brian knew they had no chance of forcing their way past three beefy camels.

'So if you're not archaeologists and you're not tomb raiders, what are you then?' challenged Tammy. 'Hairdressers?'

The camel's lips moved around into something that looked a bit like a smile in the dim light. 'Firstly, I must introduce myself properly. My true name – my *secret* name – is Cam-Ho-Tep.'

'Cam-Ho-Tep Braider?' asked Tammy.

'Don't be so stupid!' snapped the camel. 'Cam-Ho-Tep Williams. The name Tom Braider was just my little joke . . .'

Brian thought this over, then exclaimed, 'Oh, I get it! Tom Braider! TOMB RAIDER!'

He looked across at Tammy. 'Well, you have to admit, it is quite clever . . . you know, in an evil way.'

'I am the leader of the Ancient Order of Nokankumin,' continued Cam-Ho-Tep. 'For centuries our hidden society has passed down our secret from one generation to the next, always waiting for this moment . . . for the return of the King of Camel Kings! It finally became possible when Howard Oinks-Gruntington discovered the lost Hump of Doom!'

While he was talking, Dick and Drom had carried the stone camel statue into the chamber. The stone Hump still sat on top of it, its black surface glowing with a strange sort of dark light.

'And now our wait is over,' announced Cam-Ho-Tep. 'It is time for the ancient powers within this hump to work their magic.'

The two camels set the statue in the middle of the room and took a step back. All eyes were on the Hump of Doom. For a moment everything was silent, and it felt like a *something-really-really-bad-is-about-to-happen* kind of silence.

And then something really, really bad *did* happen – or at least, it did if you think that the front lid of a stone coffin creaking open is bad . . .

. . . which it was.

Because as the lid opened wider, Tammy and Brian could see the body of an ancient mummy, covered from head to toe in bandages. It let out a horrible moan and began to step out of its stone prison.

The lids of the other coffins began to
swing open too, and soon the chamber
was filled with the awful moans of several
mummies. They sounded like the world's
worst male-voice choir warming up, and the
two PiPs didn't wait to find out what they
might sing.

They spun round and raced into the
nearest open passageway behind them. This
led into another underground tunnel, but
there was no clearly marked EXIT sign –
the health-and-safety record of the ancient
Camels had been terrible. The pigs ran past
the entrance to one chamber and then on
into another.

'It's a dead end!' cried Brian.

There was a big stone table in the room and the two pigs hid behind it.

'Are you OK, Bri?' asked Tammy.

The PiPs medical officer was shaking like a leaf – a leaf that has just been chased by several scary mummies.

'I'm sure there's some perfectly sensible scientific explanation,' Brian began. He blinked rapidly. 'But it was scary back there . . . At times like this, one almost wishes one was a small piglet again, in the arms of one's mother.'

'Eh?' said Tammy.

Brian frowned. 'It's just that such moments of extreme fear are enough to make me wish I was back with my dear old mama.'

'Brian, WHAT are you going on about?' Tammy glanced over the top of the stone table.

The medical officer sighed. 'Just that . . . I want my –'

'MUMMY!' cried Tammy.

'Exactly!' said Brian, going a deeper shade of pink around the cheeks.

'No!' shouted Tammy. 'I mean there's a *mummy* at the door, and it's coming this way!'

CHAPTER 10:

Wrapping Things Up

Brian stuck his head up and saw it was true. One of the mummies was shuffling towards them with arms outstretched. It didn't look like the sort of mummy that would make you jam sandwiches with no crusts and then read you a night-night story; this one looked more like the sort of mummy that would wrap its dusty hands round your neck and squeeze very hard indeed until your eyeballs popped out. It gave an awful groan and there was a sudden whiff of centuries-old dead air.

'Ooh, mummy breath!' cried Tammy,

waving a trotter over her snout. 'GROSS!'

As Tammy and Brian burst out of their hiding-place, the mechanic dashed to the left and the medic went right. The mummy was confused – which one to grab?

This moment's confusion allowed the two pigs to duck under its outstretched arms and run back into the tunnel. They could see another mummy filling the doorway into the main burial room, so they nipped quickly into the other little room they had passed. They knew they didn't have long before another mummy found them.

'I've got an idea!' Tammy cried, kneeling and digging into her backpack. 'Here!' She pulled out a family pack of toilet paper. This was the 'special desert provisions' she had brought. 'We can wrap ourselves up so we look like mummies, too!' she explained, ripping the pack open.

'Won't we be the wrong colour?' Brian

asked. 'You don't get many mummies in lavender-coloured wrapping.'

Tammy tilted the label towards him. 'I don't get the Luxury Lavender "Feel the Difference on Your Botty" Super-Soft Loo Paper any more. I buy the Economy Grey Value-Pack "Wipe Yer Bum" Bog Paper now – it's cheaper AND it's the perfect colour for mummy bandages! Stand still, Bri – I'm about to mummify you!'

She began to wrap the first roll round the medic's leg.

'Tammy, I know there isn't time to waste, but I *must* ask . . . *why*? *Why* do you have a family pack of toilet paper in your backpack?'

Tammy didn't stop wrapping. 'You never know when you might need some loo paper, especially when you're travelling abroad to a hot island like this . . . DUH! I thought you were supposed to be clever, Brian!'

Soon she had wrapped the medic from head to toe in the grey tissue paper, with just narrow slits for eyes.

'You look great!' said Tammy. 'Now practise walking like a mummy.'

She gave a quick demonstration and Brian did his best to copy.

'I think it needs to be a bit more of a shambling shuffle,' Tammy advised, starting

to wrap herself up too. 'Drag your back foot a bit more. Also, it might help if you put your arms out in front of you, not on your hips.' She watched his second attempt. 'Yes, that's better . . . a bit. Also, you've got to groan, like this . . .' Tammy let out a low groan that echoed around the underground chamber.

'UUUUUHHHHHHHHHHHHHHH!'

Brian gave it a go. 'Aheeeeeeeeeerrm?'

'You sound like you're trying to remember your nineteen-times table.'

'The nineteen-times table is simple,' said Brian, puzzled.

'OK . . .' said Tammy, thinking fast. 'Imagine you'd just eaten my usual Saturday lunch.'

Brian had often watched in astonishment at weekends as Tammy polished off four pies, two pizzas and as many pasties as she could carry, all washed down with a bucket of Slurpo-Pop. Just the thought of it made his tummy complain.

'UUHHHH!' he moaned.

'That's it!' encouraged Tammy. 'Just keep that noise up, and maybe we can get out of here in one piece!'

She was completely wrapped up now too. She gave Brian a little nod and they both mummy-walked out of the chamber, back towards the burial room.

'How far have we gone now?' groaned Pete.

'About seven miles,' Howard said.

'Seven point six!' corrected Peregrine instantly.

Howard would normally have argued, but both pigs were too hot and tired even to bicker. Whoever was right, they had still gone less than halfway. How would they ever make it to the Valley of the Camel Kings?

Out in front, Curly plodded over yet another dune . . . and then stopped. He could see a tall robed figure in the distance, just looking at him. His first thought was that this was another mirage, and yet so far all of the mirages had involved quenching your thirst. Maybe this strange figure in the desert was *real*?

'Coo-ee!' Curly waved. 'Hello! Can you help us, please?'

The figure didn't respond in any way.

The other pigs had caught up with Curly by now.

'Can you see it too?' the trainee asked.

'We can.' Peregrine raised his voice. 'Who ARE you?'

Still no answer, but the tall figure lifted one trotter, and a slender pig's arm – well, slender by pig standards – emerged from its white robes. It pointed at something large and half buried in the sand.

With their last dregs of energy, the pigs staggered over and began to brush the sand off this object.

'I think it's . . . yes! It's an aeroplane!' exclaimed Pete.

'I've never seen one like *this* before!' said Curly.

It was nothing like the zappy, top-of-the-line SkyHog jets the Pigs in Planes zoomed around in. This plane was much, much older. It still had a propeller at the front, and on each side it had two wings, one on top of the other, separated by a network of thin struts.

'It must have been here for a hundred years or more,' said Howard.

But Peregrine was looking at the wrecked plane with an odd misty expression in his eyes. 'It's beautiful,' he said. 'It's a Sopwith Camel. They were old, even when I started flying, but I was lucky enough to do some training in one. They fly like a dream!'

'This one looks more like a nightmare,'
said Pete. 'It's been here for so long, it's just a
piece of rusted old junk.'

Peregrine turned towards the far-off
figure, who just gave a slow nod of the head.

'How mysterious,' said Curly.

'That's one word for it,' said Pete. 'Others
are *weird* and *really sort of creepy*.'

Moments later, a wind came from
nowhere. It blew stronger and stronger,

hurling hot sand into the air until
the four pigs were unable to see
anything, while their faces and
bodies were sand-blasted.

Curly tried to shout, 'Sand
is getting in my mouth!' but
he couldn't because sand was
getting in his mouth.

If it carried on like this much
longer, they were going to find
themselves buried up to their
necks in sand once again . . .

CHAPTER 11:

Pharaoh Frenzy

Tammy and Brian shuffled back to the
main burial chamber in their mummy
disguises. Most of the other mummies
were still there. Both they and the three
living camels were all gazing at the big
sarcophagus in the centre of the room. The
black stone Hump on the camel statue
seemed to be glowing even more. They
could feel the crackle of some unseen energy
in the air.

Nervous that their loo-roll disguises
would be seen through, Tammy started
towards the exit. Brian followed. Nobody

grabbed them or tried to rip their fake bandages off. But then one of the real mummies placed a cold hand on Tammy's shoulder and slowly turned her round towards the centre of the room. Another mummy did the same to Brian.

All of the mummies had linked arms to watch what was going on in the middle of the stone room. With the mummies' vice-like grips on their shoulders, Tammy and Brian could do nothing but watch too.

The big sarcophagus was open now. Inside, with its arms folded across its narrow chest, lay the dried-up body of a camel. It wore a tall pharaoh's hat and there were golden symbols all over its faded robes. These were the remains of the Great Pharaoh Nokankumin.

The body looked as if it had been in there an awfully long time, but with each passing second, it was changing. The air in the chamber felt charged with power as the pharaoh's wrinkled flesh began to fill out and look less leathery. In general, it was looking less ancient . . . less dried-up . . . altogether less *DEAD*.

In fact, after a few more seconds, it was looking really quite alive, especially when its long eyelashes fluttered and its cold yellow eyes snapped open.

Then it sat up for the first time in several thousand years. It looked around and produced an evil, thin-lipped smile. Cam-Ho-Tep and his helpers started bowing down. The mummies were doing this as well, and so Tammy and Brian quickly copied them.

When the pharaoh spoke, his voice was like the wind through an ancient dusty tomb, or perhaps like a really old camel with a tickly cough.

'I have returned!' said Nokankumin,

King of Camel Kings. 'And after so long in that sarcophagus, I am in a *very* bad mood indeed!'

The sudden desert wind stopped as quickly as it had started. When it did, the four exhausted pigs saw that the sand covering the Sopwith Camel biplane had been blown away. That wasn't all – it had gone from being a half-buried wreck to looking like an exhibit in an aeroplane museum.

'Incredible!' said Pete. 'But I still don't

see how it helps us. I mean, it won't be able to go anywhere, will it? After all this time, surely there's no fuel in the tank.'

Peregrine had clambered up to the open cockpit. 'You're right, it's completely empty,' he said, tapping the fuel gauge sadly. As soon as he did this, the gauge's needle slowly moved to the right. 'Erm, wait – what I meant is, it's *completely full!*'

The mysterious robed pig was still watching them silently from a distance.

'OK, but there's no way the propeller's ever going to turn,' said Pete. To prove his point, he gave the plane's propeller a spin. It whizzed round as if it was brand new. The ancient aeroplane's engine rumbled into instant life.

'Get on!' shouted the wing commander from the pilot's seat. 'I do believe she's going to fly!' There was only space for one more pig in the cockpit, so Howard wedged himself behind his big brother. Curly had to crouch on one of the lower wings and grip on to the struts that separated it from the upper wing.

The sudden wind had uncovered a runway, too, and the only things stopping the plane from zooming along this now were two wooden blocks – known as *chocks* – placed in front of the wheels. Once these were pulled away, the plane would start to move. The only person who could do this was Pete, and then he'd have to hop nimbly up on to the other wing before the plane got up too much speed.

Peregrine was beaming as he readied himself to shout two words he thought he'd never get to say again.

'CHOCKS AWAY!'

CHAPTER 12:

The Plan Unravels

Tammy and Brian weren't having much luck making their escape from the burial room. Every time either of them took a mummy-step towards the tunnel out of the chamber, something seemed to get in the way.

Meanwhile, the newly revived Pharaoh Nokankumin was getting used to being alive again.

'Soon I will establish myself once more as ruler of this world and the next,' he declared grandly. An annoyed look crossed his face. 'But first, I want this place tidied up. I can't stand a messy tomb. You there!' He pointed at one of the smaller mummies. 'Make yourself useful and close all the sarcophagi lids!'

The mummy started towards the first stone coffin. From the safety of her own disguise, Tammy watched nervously. Only she knew that the mummy walking around the room's edge was actually Brian Trotter.

But the medic was doing his best to act like a mummy. He let out one or two dreadful groans as he closed the first lid and shuffled towards the next sarcophagus.

That's when Tammy noticed something terrible. The loo paper round Brian's leg had begun to unwind. A loose end was flapping down about one ankle. He didn't know it, but with each shuffling mummy-step the PiPs medic took, more paper unwound. Soon the trousers of his uniform would be visible.

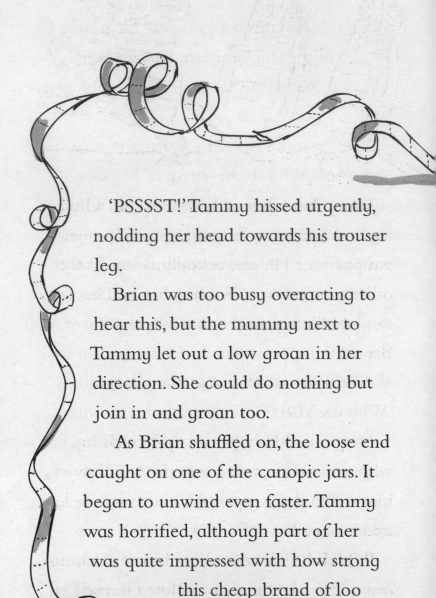

'PSSSST!' Tammy hissed urgently, nodding her head towards his trouser leg.

Brian was too busy overacting to hear this, but the mummy next to Tammy let out a low groan in her direction. She could do nothing but join in and groan too.

As Brian shuffled on, the loose end caught on one of the canopic jars. It began to unwind even faster. Tammy was horrified, although part of her was quite impressed with how strong this cheap brand of loo paper was.

Brian didn't have a clue that one whole leg and half of his tummy were no longer wrapped up. The groans and moans of the other mummies in the chamber had become more baffled. Everybody was watching Brian.

'STOP!' cried Pharaoh Nokankumin. 'Who are YOU?'

He pointed his golden crook at Brian, who was still unaware that the only bits of him still under wraps were his arms, one leg and his head.

'UUHHHH!' he said in his best mummy-groan. He silently congratulated himself on how *mummyish* he sounded.

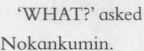'WHAT?' asked
Nokankumin.

'I said . . . UHHH,'
replied Brian. 'You
know, like a mummy?'
He looked at the
real mummies all
staring at him. 'Oops.'
Then he looked down
at his exposed flightsuit.
'Double oops!'

Then he looked back
at the trail of unwound
loo paper on the floor
behind him. Before
he could even say
'Triple oops!' the
camels Dick and
Drom grabbed hold
of him.

Nokankumin

speared the PiPs medic with his most evil glare. 'You will have the honour of witnessing the rebirth of my mighty empire,' he hissed.

'Just a sec, O mighty King of Camel Kings!' cried Cam-Ho-Tep. 'There were TWO pigs, master. Perhaps another of your faithful servants here is an imposter?'

Nokankumin glared at the assembled mummies. He raised a dried-out eyebrow and commanded, 'All of you, turn to the side.'

The mummies obeyed. Brian guessed that the pharaoh was checking to see if any of them *didn't* have a hump at the back. The mummies' humps were much smaller than those of living camels, but they were still noticeable.

And yet there didn't seem to be a mummy in the room WITHOUT a hump. That was because Tammy was still wearing her backpack underneath her loo-roll bandages!

Nokankumin's eyes narrowed to slits. 'Now say something,' he ordered the mummies.

He pointed to each in turn and, one by one, they let out a low mummy groan. They all sounded the same. Even Brian wasn't sure now which one was Tammy. Or maybe NONE of the mummies was Tammy? Maybe she'd managed to sneak away?

'Very well,' scowled Nokankumin. 'Time for a break . . . Who'd like a bit of cake?'

Immediately, the arm of just one mummy – a short, round mummy – shot up into the air. It fell again as soon as its owner looked around the room, but it was too late.

Nokankumin pressed his thin lips into a cruel smirk. 'Get that *pig*,' he snarled.

'Yes, master!' cried Cam-Ho-Tep eagerly.

Before Tammy could do anything, the camel once known as Tom was holding her arm in an iron grip. With her free trotter, she pulled away the loo paper from her face. 'OK, you've got me,' she said. 'But do I still get that bit of cake?'

The pharaoh's eyes blazed. 'By the time you see what I've got planned, you won't be in the mood for CAKE!' He threw his head back for a good old classic evil laugh. With centuries of tomb dust in his throat, this soon became a series of dry coughs.

'Are you OK, O Great One? Um . . . can I get you a drink?' offered Cam-Ho-Tep.

'No!' croaked Nokankumin. 'Just bring me the Hump of Doom! The time has come for me to summon my Armies of the Undead!'

Tammy and Brian swapped nervous looks. They weren't sure what the pharaoh was going on about, but one thing was certain – it did not sound like a pleasant way to spend the afternoon.

CHAPTER 13:

Hump Day

Nokankumin's long bony arms quivered with excitement as he reached out for the Hump of Doom. As soon as his hooves closed round it and lifted it, there was a deafening sizzle, like a massive power surge all around the chamber. Blue lightning seemed to spark and flash out of the Hump itself. The walls began to rumble and shake again, much worse than before.

'The time has come!' screamed Nokankumin. 'Let Hump Day begin!'

Rocks and stone blocks were falling all around them now, and Tammy had an odd feeling in her stomach — the sort of feeling you get when you're in a lift going up. The reason for this was simple — they WERE going *up*. The very stone floor beneath their feet was zooming upwards.

However, it didn't hurtle into the tomb's ceiling because the stone blocks above them were crashing and breaking to reveal bright blue sky. The sides of the floor seemed to fall away as the flagstone at its

centre point shot upwards. The rest of the tomb followed. Brian and Tammy found themselves clinging to moving blocks of stone and squinting against the sudden glare of sunlight all around them.

Tammy looked over her shoulder and realized that they were on top of a great pyramid. It must have been there all along, buried underneath the hidden tomb of Nokankumin. Somehow, the frenzied pharaoh had used the power of the Hump to bring it bursting up out of the rock and sand.

Now Nokankumin stood on the highest stone of the pyramid, holding the Hump of Doom up in his reedy arms.

'Come, my Armies of the Undead!' he cried. 'Hump Day is here! It is time to claim this world again for the glory of the Great Pharaoh Nokankumin!'

There was a booming noise from further

down one side of the pyramid.

'What's THAT?' shouted Tammy.

'I'm only guessing,' cried Brian, 'but I'd say that's the sound of his Armies of the Undead turning up!'

The Sopwith Camel biplane was zooming low across the desert. On either side, Pete and Curly held on tight to the wings' struts.

'Who do you think she was?' cried Curly. 'That pig back there?'

'Don't know!' roared Peregrine into the wind. 'But she certainly knew her vintage planes!'

The wing commander was in hog heaven, his immense moustache fluttering in the wind like a proud flag made entirely of facial hair. In his opinion, this was *proper* flying – much better than all your fancy jet engines and new-fangled, namby-pamby computer systems.

Sitting behind him, Howard was considerably less happy to be up in the air. Pale with fear, he gripped the back of Peregrine's seat and stared intently at his own trotters, while trying not to be sick on his brother's head.

Peregrine bellowed over the roar of the propeller. 'So, Howard, is this valley of yours anywhere near that pyramid?'

'There IS no pyramid in this part of the desert,' his younger brother replied, not looking up.

Peregrine gave a scoffing laugh. 'You can't be a very good archaeologist, Howard! I'm no expert, but that enormous, pointy triangular thingy over there looks like a pyramid to me.'

Howard forced himself to look up and past his big brother's hefty shoulder. He couldn't believe his eyes – there it was, a huge stone pyramid, in a spot where before

there had been no pyramid.

'That's not all,' yelled Peregrine. 'There are some animals on top of that pyramid . . . and I think two of them are Tammy and Brian!'

'And THAT'S not all!' yelled Curly, still holding on tight. 'There's some sort of great big door opening in the side of the pyramid and lots of creepy-looking mummies getting ready to come out of it!'

The pigs on the biplane watched in astonishment. It didn't look like an actual doorway so much as a kind of gigantic hole in time and space. Through it, a sea of mummies – thousands of them – shambled towards the sunlight.

Pete just shrugged. 'Well, that's not something you see every day,' he murmured.

Peregrine was flying the plane straight towards the top of the pyramid now. Behind him, Howard quickly took in the situation. 'That strange-looking camel is Nokankumin!' he gasped in amazement.

'How can that be?' cried Curly.

'I don't know,' said the archaeologist. 'But I'm pretty sure of one thing – we have to get that Hump away from him!'

On top of the pyramid, Tammy and Brian couldn't believe their ears when they heard the buzz of an aeroplane. Seconds later they saw it, zooming across the sands. Although it wasn't a SkyHog, Tammy had a feeling that the other PiPs were here to help out.

Waves of energy were coming from the Hump of Doom in the pharaoh's hands. Whatever its mysterious power was, it seemed much, much stronger when Nokankumin was holding it . . .

'POWER!' cried the pharaoh. 'I feel it, stronger and stronger with each passing second! Soon the Hump will be strong enough, and the gate between worlds will be flung open! BWA-HA-HA –' Again his evil laugh ended in an evil coughing fit.

A roaring sound was coming from the Hump now, and because of this din, the pharaoh didn't hear the sound of the approaching plane. Tammy saw that Peregrine was at the controls and Pete was flat on his tummy on one lower wing, leaning down with his trotters out at the ready.

She understood in an instant – he was going to try to grab the Hump. But would he be able to pull it from the iron grip of the mad pharaoh?

Tammy had to help. Pulling free from the mummy who held her, she jumped up a stone block and leapt for the Hump, hoping to dislodge it from Nokankumin's grip.

'How dare you lay a trotter on the Camel King of Kings!' cried Nokankumin.

The pharaoh held out one arm to keep her away, while he held the Hump higher with his other arm. His mummy guards were moving towards him. They too had seen the fast-approaching plane now and they were rushing to protect their master. Brian also charged forward to help his team-mate.

They all met in a giant scrum at the top of the pyramid, with everyone making a grab for the Hump of Doom. Then the air was filled with the sound of the biplane's propeller as the aircraft whizzed overhead.

It was an *almost* perfect bit of flying by Peregrine. There was just one problem – he didn't quite fly the plane high enough to clear the tallest of the mummies. The Sopwith Camel's tail slammed into it, and this mummy smashed right into the rest of the group on top of the pyramid. All of them – pigs, pharaoh and mummies – began to fall down the stone steps. They barrelled

right into the three camels who had helped
to bring the pharaoh back to life. As they
all tumbled down to the bottom, Brian and
Tammy made most of the noise –

'**OO!**

OW!

OUCH!

WAAH!

OOH!

OOF!'

– all the way to the foot of the pyramid,
where they landed in a huge pile. Luckily,
Dick and Drom reached the bottom first
and broke the others' fall.

Nokankumin sat up and straightened his pharaoh hat. Then he fixed Tammy and Brian with an evil glare.

'Where is my Hump?' he spat.

Tammy just pointed a trotter up to the blue skies above. 'My friend Pete's got it,' she said with a defiant smile.

Nokankumin turned to one of his servants. 'Dispose of these pigs, mummy,' he snarled. 'My other mummy will soon bring me the Hump.'

Tammy glanced upwards at the plane in alarm. It was true – Pete had managed to grab the Hump, but that wasn't the only thing from the top of the pyramid that was now on the plane.

CHAPTER 14:

Battle in the Sky

As Peregrine pulled away from the top of the pyramid, he was feeling pretty pleased with his piloting skills. Most importantly, Pete had the Hump! Peregrine gave a thumbs-up to the captain.

'I think we need to throw the Hump into that big portal thingy!' cried Howard into the wind.

'Why's that?' asked Peregrine. 'Did you read it in an ancient scroll or something?'

'No,' answered Howard. 'I saw it in a movie!'

Suddenly, a cry came from the other wing: 'Help!'

Peregrine looked over and saw
Curly cowering against the side of
the plane as a huge mummy crawled
towards him. *A mummy! On the
plane!* It must have caught on to the
wing and hauled itself aboard when
Pete had grabbed the Hump.

Anger surged through Peregrine.
*I'll show that mummy who the daddy
is!* he thought.

'Hold on tight, PiPs!' he shouted,
and he threw the plane into a
corkscrew spin over the desert.

When he levelled off again, he saw that his stunt-flying had worked – it had shaken someone right off the wing. Unfortunately, it wasn't the mummy, but *Curly* who had failed to hold on tight. The PiPs trainee had tumbled and landed in a sand dune below with a dull *THUD*!

Meanwhile, the mummy on the wing was heading for the cockpit. Peregrine was about to try to shake it off again, when Pete shouted across from the other wing.

'Oi, mummy!' He held the stone Hump up in one trotter. 'If you want this, come and get it!' Then he clambered up on to the top wing. Immediately, the mummy climbed up too, on the other side of the plane.

Now the two of them were on the top wing. The mummy let out a fearsome moan as it shuffled towards Pete.

'Back off, mummy!' the captain growled,

sounding like the world's worst-mannered child.

'UHHHHHHH!' the mummy groaned as it made a grab for the Hump of Doom. The two began to grapple. Pete was one tough hog, but it wasn't easy competing with the forces of ancient evil. Also, the mummy was bigger and stronger. It gave Pete a mighty shove. The pig staggered backwards. Then he staggered back some more, but now he had run out of wing – he staggered right off the edge, and suddenly he was freefalling through the air, still clutching the Hump. He was hurtling towards the rocky clifftops of the Valley of the Camel Kings. 'Whoah!'

But he didn't go *SPLAT*! In the struggle, one of the mummy's bandages had got tangled round Pete. As he fell, this bandage unwound and unwound until it reached its full length, leaving Pete dangling helplessly below the biplane.

'Pig overboard!' cried Peregrine, and he furiously angled the plane to shake the intruder off. The mummy staggered backwards along the top wing, unable to keep its footing. Then it too fell off. The bandage that attached it to Pete still didn't break; it pulled tight so that as the mummy fell, Pete shot upwards.

Now the PiPs captain was hanging down on one side of the plane and the mummy was hanging down on the other, with the bandage that connected them looped up and over the main part of the plane.

Under the strain of all this extra weight, the plane's engine was beginning to cough and sputter. It wouldn't be able to fly much longer. Pete knew he had to do something – and fast. The mummy hanging on the other side was swinging towards him, its dead grey eyes fixed on the Hump of Doom in his arms.

'UUUHHHHHH!' groaned the mummy.

'You've already said that!' answered Pete.

The mummy swooped closer and closer, arms outstretched. There was no way Pete could avoid it . . .

He looked down at the sand below and then he let go of the Hump.

CHAPTER 15:

The Oinks-Gruntingtons United

Brian and Tammy were charging across the desert away from the pyramid.

They weren't exactly sure what Nokankumin had meant by his order to 'dispose of the pigs', but they weren't keen to find out.

Brian glanced over his shoulder. Several of the mummies were chasing, but their strange shuffling walk wasn't the most efficient way to move across sand at speed.

Unfortunately, something else was chasing them too – something much faster. Although his two assistants were still lying in an unconscious heap at the foot of the pyramid, Cam-Ho-Tep was galloping after them.

'Faster!' shouted Brian.

Tammy looked at the expanse of sand in front of her. 'Er . . . *where*?'

The biplane swept into view across the horizon in front of them. The glare of the sun made it hard to see clearly, but it looked as if something was hanging down underneath it. Behind them, the sound of camel hoofsteps grew louder.

Suddenly, something fell from the plane and landed in the sand ahead of them.

'What's *that*?' cried Tammy.

Brian squinted. 'I think it's –'

'The Hump!' cried Cam-Ho-Tep, catching up with the two pigs and grinning evilly. 'Now nothing can stop us!'

This wasn't exactly true. Up until this moment, Pete and the mummy were perfectly balanced as they dangled under the plane. But as soon as Pete let go of the Hump, this meant the mummy was much heavier. So Pete shot up towards the plane while the mummy dropped lower.

This final drop was too much for the bandage, which was several thousand years old, after all. It snapped and the mummy fell to the sands below.

In fact, it landed right on top of Tammy, Brian and Cam-Ho-Tep,

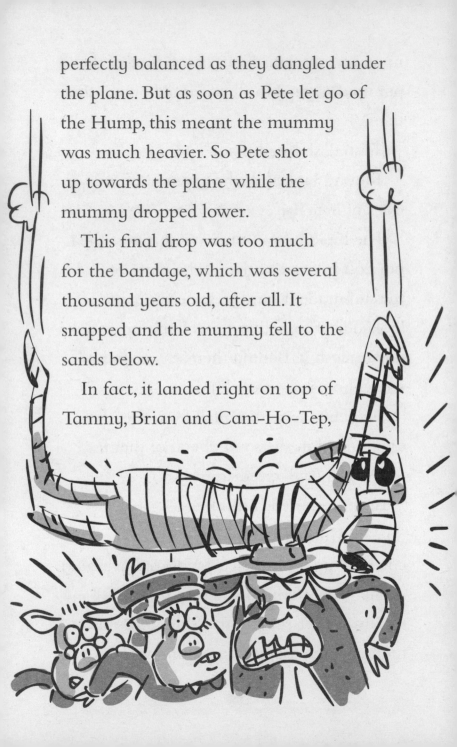

just a second and a half after the camel had said, 'Nothing can stop us now!'

Up in the air, Peregrine could see that the situation down on the sand wasn't looking good. The Hump was just lying there in the sand, but neither Brian nor Tammy seemed to be moving. Nor was Cam-Ho-Tep, and for the same reason (a falling mummy on the head).

However, the mummies that had also been chasing the two pigs continued to shamble towards the Hump. Nokankumin was already striding out from the pyramid to join them.

'What now?' cried Peregrine. 'Any suggestions, Captain?'

Peter Porker was back on the lower wing, but something wasn't right with him. He just smiled strangely and said, 'I like rainbows.'

'Oh no! He bashed his head when

he bounced back up to the plane!' cried Peregrine. 'What are we going to do now?'

There was nobody to answer his question now except Howard, and what good was he? His kid brother always had his head in the sand.

And yet . . . the archaeologist started clambering out of the cockpit on to the lower wing.

'Get ready to fly by for the Hump!' he told his big brother.

Peregrine understood – his brother was going to leap down and get the Hump himself. There was only one thing to say: 'Good luck, Howard.'

Howard nodded. Peregrine brought the plane lower, almost skimming across the desert now.

'And don't mess up!' added the wing commander as Howard leapt down into the highest dune. He landed head first in the sand.

Pulling his head out as quickly as he could, he scanned the desert. The pharaoh's mummies were shuffling closer and closer towards the Hump. Gritting his teeth, Howard ran as fast as his trotters would carry him. He had to stop Nokankumin from getting his dried-up hands on that Hump again. More importantly, he had to prove to Peregrine that he could do this.

The first of the mummies was almost at the Hump. Howard put on a final burst of speed. He dived towards the Hump, scooping it in his arms and rolling clear of the mummy.

As he scrambled to his feet, he saw that he was too late. The other mummies had surrounded him.

'UUHHHH!' they said in a way that seemed to mean, 'Got you!'

Nokankumin had almost joined them now. The pharaoh's dried-up face twisted into an expression of evil gloating. 'I believe that's my Hump,' he sneered. 'If you'll do the honours, mummy?'

The biggest of the mummies wrenched the Hump from Howard's trotters. It was as easy as taking candy – ancient, *evil* candy – from a baby.

Howard could hear the plane above getting ready to swing round and fly by. It didn't even matter. What was the point now? The mummies had the Hump.

However, the plane held its course. Could Peregrine see what was going on? What did his big brother expect him to do? Rip the Hump back from the mummy's hands?

Howard didn't see what he could do, unless . . .

As the roar of the plane grew louder, he sprang at the mummy. It tightened its vice-like grip on the Hump. But Howard wasn't reaching for the Hump, he was reaching for the bandage that had come loose and was hanging down from the mummy's side. Working fast, he tied the end of it into a loop and then, as the plane roared past overhead, he tossed the loop up. It went right over the plane's tail.

As the plane zipped up and away, the bandage unravelled. This made the mummy spin, whirling round and round like a gigantic spinning top. It whizzed round faster and faster, its features a blur, blasting showers of sand in every direction.

'Get the Hump!' shrieked Nokankumin to the other mummies.

As an archaeologist, there were so many questions Howard had for a real pharaoh, but under the circumstances he could think of just one thing to say to the wrinkled, ancient camel: 'Oh, pipe down, prune-features!'

The spinning mummy was going faster and faster, until . . . at last, the force became too much and it was unable to hold on to the Hump of Doom. The lump of stone shot out like a cannonball, just missing Howard's head. It blasted off over the desert in the direction of the plane, which Peregrine had already begun to turn in a tight circle. Still sitting out on the wing, Pete was letting his trotters dangle over the edge and was humming lullabies.

'OOF!' The Hump landed right in his arms.

When he'd caught his breath, Pete looked down with a dazed smile. 'Is it a present? Is it my birthday?'

CHAPTER 16:

Wind and Ice

All Peregrine could think of was something
Howard had said: they had to throw that
Hump into the giant portal on the pyramid.

Would it work? He didn't know, but it was
worth a try. Peregrine started flying right
towards the doorway. Through the other side
they could see thousands of mummies in
the darkness – Nokankumin's Armies of the
Undead, still waiting to march out.

'Get ready to throw the Hump!' shouted
Peregrine.

'But it's a present for me,' smiled Pete, still
completely out of it after his bash to the head.

Peregrine thought fast. 'It's a woolly hat, Pete!' he cried. 'An UNCOOL woolly hat. Throw it!'

This message got through to the captain, who hurled the Hump with all his might. At the same time, Peregrine threw the plane into a steep climb. The Hump of Doom plopped right into the portal creating lots of zappy lights that would have made brilliant special effects in a movie.

'Wheeee!' cried Pete,

enjoying the plane ride as if he was on a rollercoaster.

As soon as the Hump disappeared, it was as if a switch had been thrown. But this switch didn't click the lights on – it triggered a gale-force wind that seemed to suck everything back towards the portal like the world's most lethally powerful vacuum cleaner.

The biplane wobbled, but held its course. Down on the ground, the same was not true for the mummies or their pharaoh leader. They seemed powerless to stop themselves from being pulled back towards the giant portal.

Howard felt himself swept along too. He slammed right into Tammy and Brian, who were just waking up to find themselves in the middle of a sandstorm.

'Grab my trotter!' cried Brian.

The pigs huddled together, holding on to

Cam-Ho-Tep and doing their best to keep their feet on the ground.

Nokankumin tumbled past them through the air.

'Oh, it's just not fair, oh!' cried the pharaoh helplessly. 'I want my mummies!'

As the sandstorm became stronger and stronger, the pigs could feel their trotters lifting off the ground. Any moment now and they would be sucked towards the giant doorway too.

But then, over the roar of the wind, came the jaunty sound of chimes. A squarish shape appeared through the sandstorm. It was an ice-cream van! An ice-cream van with a picture of a penguin on the side!

Curly was hanging out of the open hatch, with a lolly in one trotter. 'It wasn't a mirage!' he cried. 'It's *real*! They picked me up after I fell out of the plane!'

The other PiPs and the camel huddled

behind the bulk of the parked ice-cream van and looked towards the pyramid. They were just in time to see Nokankumin and his mummies disappear into the portal. Its shape and size no longer looked stable. At the same time, the pyramid was beginning to buckle and collapse in on itself. Great stone blocks crumbled and fell as the structure returned to the timeless sand.

When the enormous cloud of dust settled at last, there was no sign that any of it had ever been there. The pyramid, the pharaoh and his mummies were all gone. Apart from the buzz of Peregrine's plane, silence returned to the desert.

'Where do you think they've gone?' asked Howard.

'Who knows?' shrugged Tammy. 'But at least Nokankumin's with all his mummies.'

'So who wants an ice lolly?' piped up Curly.

A penguin poked its head out of the
hatch. 'You still haven't paid for the one
you've got, pal,' it said.

Up overhead, Peregrine threw the
Sopwith Camel into a victory roll.

Before the PiPs could leave, they waited for
the Camel Island police so they could hand
over the members of the Ancient Order of
Nokankumin.

'We've waited all our lives to bring the

pharaoh back,' said Cam-Ho-Tep bleakly. 'What are we going to do now? Our lives have no purpose.'

Tammy thought this over. 'You probably ought to take up a new hobby,' she said. 'You can think of one when you're in jail.'

Now that Brian had looked at his head, Pete was feeling OK again (although he refused to have any bandages on it in case they ruined his hairstyle).

'There's just one thing I don't understand,' said Pete. 'Who was that mysterious pig in the desert? The one who showed us the biplane?'

Brian gave him a wide-eyed stare as he put away his medical kit. There were *hundreds* of things about this mission that the PiPs medic didn't understand.

'I've got another question,' said Tammy. 'How did you even get that old pile of junk in the air?'

She pointed across the sand to where the biplane lay. Once again it looked like a total wreck. There was no way something in that condition could ever budge the slightest bit, let alone fly across the desert to the rescue.

'Maybe we could ask the nice lady,' piped up Curly, slurping his eleventh ice lolly. 'She's over there!'

The other pigs looked towards the dune the young trainee was pointing at. The robed pig was there, looking impossibly tall with the setting sun behind her. She pulled back the hood and smiled at the PiPs for just a moment. The sun at her back seemed to shine even brighter, dazzling the pigs. When their eyes adjusted, the mysterious figure was gone.

'That was weird,' said Tammy.

Brian just blinked. He looked again at the setting sun, and then shook his head in disbelief. Sometimes it was better to say nothing, and so he did not tell the others that the pig on the dune had looked exactly like the hieroglyphic symbol of the ancient pig-headed goddess Hamm.

EPILOGUE

While the others flew back to HQ, Peregrine dropped Howard off on Pig Island. The two brothers shook trotters for the first time in years.

'So what are you going to do now?' beamed Peregrine fondly. 'You can hardly put your head back in the sand after all that, can you?'

Howard bristled. 'What, I suppose I ought to grow a moustache like yours and swan about in the skies, should I?'

'Don't be silly,' said Peregrine. 'You could *never* grow a fine moustache like mine.'

'Only a fat old walrus would want to grow a moustache like that.'

And so on.

Before they parted, the last words Howard said were, 'Big Nose'. The last words Peregrine said were, 'Chicken Legs'. It was an odd way for brothers to get on, but it was the way of the Oinks-Gruntingtons.

The other members of the PiPs were happy to return to the steady drizzle of Snout Island.

Only Brian still looked dazed after everything that had happened. 'There was a scientific explanation for it all, of course there was,' he mumbled to himself as they went inside. 'No such thing as ancient gods or magic. It probably has something to do with black holes causing time and space to bend and . . . Yes, that's it! It wasn't *magic*, it was just PHYSICS at work!'

As he rambled on, he didn't hear the footsteps behind him. Something tapped him on the shoulder and he turned to look right into the bandaged face of another mummy.

'WAAAAAAAAAAAAAAAAAAAAAAAA-AAAAAAAAAH!' yelled Brian, the pig of science. He tore out of the common room faster than a cheetah on jet-powered roller skates.

'What's his problem?' asked Lola. 'I only wanted to show him my mummy costume for the party.' She did a little twirl. 'See — you can't notice my spot now with *this* costume!'

The other pigs were at the window, watching as Brian charged across the lawn in front of PiPs HQ. He was going so fast that he tripped and went sprawling, right into a puddle. He got up slowly and looked down at his mud-soaked trousers.

Tammy gave the others a knowing look. 'He needs to change his trousers now. See? Mystic Moggy's horoscopes are always right!'

Tammy was still chuckling about this fifteen minutes later when she had to nip to the loo. That's when she stopped laughing.

'Hello!' she shouted. 'There's no toilet paper in here! Can anyone hear me? HELLO!'

READ MORE OiNKCREDiBLY FUNNY ADVENTURES OF THE

The Chicken Egg-splosion

PAUL COOPER

The Shark Bites Back

PAUL COOPER

The Big Baad Sheep

PAUL COOPER

The Mega Monkey Mystery

PAUL COOPER

The Camel's Hump of Doom

PAUL COOPER

The Big Bear Nightmare

PAUL COOPER

www.puffin.co.uk

Wordsearch

Find the words opposite hidden in this grid.
(Look carefully – some may be
backwards or diagonal!)

N	D	N	A	U	D	A	R	C	O	L
O	A	O	N	N	C	B	H	U	M	P
K	C	I	Y	E	A	B	O	R	U	J
A	V	P	R	O	M	L	Y	S	S	I
N	U	R	O	B	E	E	M	E	W	R
K	O	O	R	A	L	S	M	L	E	C
U	P	C	C	L	I	N	U	B	A	N
M	D	S	A	N	D	E	M	O	F	Y
I	W	V	S	L	O	R	H	R	B	M
N	O	I	A	L	D	T	C	C	I	T
Y	O	R	P	O	R	T	A	L	N	O

* Turn to page 150 for the answers.

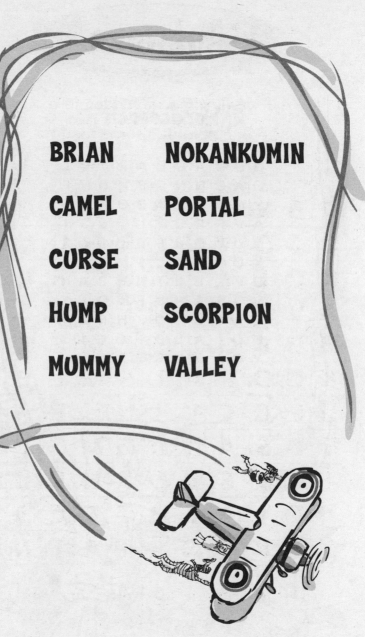

BRIAN   NOKANKUMIN

CAMEL   PORTAL

CURSE   SAND

HUMP   SCORPION

MUMMY   VALLEY

Answers

Wordsearch

N	D	N	A	U	D	A	R	C	O	L
O	A	O	N	N	C	B	H	U	M	P
K	C	I	Y	E	A	B	O	R	U	J
A	V	P	R	O	M	L	Y	S	S	I
N	U	R	O	B	E	E	M	E	W	R
K	O	O	R	A	L	S	M	L	E	C
U	P	C	C	L	I	N	U	B	A	N
M	D	S	A	N	D	E	M	O	F	Y
I	W	V	S	L	O	R	H	R	B	M
N	O	I	A	L	D	T	C	C	I	T
Y	O	R	P	O	R	T	A	L	N	O